3 On A

Moonbeam

Book Two in the
Moonbeam Series

Happy Moonbeams

By Joyce Sandilands

Illustrated by Simone Padur

A special thank you to the Vickers, Silversides, Von Salzen Families, and teacher, Trudy Robinson, for their helpful critique and support.

Whitlands Publishing Ltd.
4444 Tremblay Drive
Victoria, Canada V8N 4W5
250-477-0192
www.whitlands.com
email: info@whitlands.com

Library and Archives Canada Cataloguing in Publication

Sandilands, Joyce, 1945-
    3 on a moonbeam / Joyce Sandilands ; illustrated by Simone Padur.

(Moonbeam series ; 2)
ISBN 0-9734383-1-2

    I. Padur, Simone, 1978- II. Title. III. Title: Three on a moonbeam. IV. Series.

PS8637.A54T47 2004   jC813'.6   C2004-903527-4

Printed and bound in Canada by
Friesen Printers, Altona, Manitoba

To my granddaughter, Shayla,
for her valuable assistance on this story
and its audio book.
Such precious memories.

and

To my husband, Robert,
for his encouragement.

3 On A Moonbeam

By Joyce Sandilands

Contents

Chapter 1

Paddy, the Parade Marshall

Summer is coming to Fairyland and it's a very busy place. School will be out in just a few weeks. Then it will be time for the Fairyland Day Fair. This is a very special fair. It only comes once a year.

On the morning of the fair, there's a grand parade. The parade has fancy floats and marching bands. After, everyone goes to the fair to play games and go on rides. It's a lot of fun.

Paddy, the leprechaun, and Jake, the blue and green parrot, will both be in the parade. Many of their friends will be in the parade, too. The leprechauns have been practising for weeks. Their marching band leads the parade.

Even the ant choir has new bow-ties and hats. Everywhere you go you can hear them singing.

Paddy and Jake are best friends. They are also Moonbeam Riders. They became Moonbeam Riders when they graduated from Grade Four.

This year, the parade will be a special one for Paddy.

He is the Parade Marshall. The job of Parade Marshall is to lead the grand parade. However, Paddy has a problem. He has to learn something new to be the Parade Marshall. He's had a very hard time deciding what that will be. So he asked his friend, Jake, to help him.

"What am I going to do, Jake?" he asked. "I can't think of anything. I'm not very talented. Help me find something to do."

"Oh Paddy! You are talented. Think hard!" squawked the bird, flapping his wings.

Paddy stood with his hands on his hips and glared at Jake. "All right, if you're so smart, tell me what talent I have!"

"Well, you could do cartwheels," said Jake.

"You're being silly. You know I'm terrible at gymnastics," grunted Paddy.

"Well, how about juggling? I know you can juggle," said the parrot.

"But I'm supposed to learn something new!" groaned Paddy. "You're not much help at all. I'm going to find someone else who will help me."

Paddy set off down the street toward the park. Jake flew ahead of him. They found Paddy's cousin, Liam, having a swing. Liam is older than Paddy. He is a happy leprechaun who loves to dress up and always smiles.

Jake flew over and landed on the swing next to him.

"Hey Liam! Paddy could use your help on this parade stuff," he squawked softly. He didn't want Paddy to hear. Then he flew back to his friend.

Liam was puzzled. He wondered what Jake meant.

"Hi Paddy," called Liam. "What are you two doing?"

"Oh … nothing much," said Paddy, looking down at the ground. He kicked a stone.

Hmm, thought Liam. *Something is wrong. Let's see if I can find out what it is.* "How are your plans for the parade coming?"

"Parade? Uh … well …," began Paddy.

"Paddy, why don't you ask him?" said Jake.

"Ask me what?" asked Liam.

Paddy sighed and began to pace up and down.

"I-I don't want to be the Parade Marshall anymore. I can't think of anything to do," he said sadly.

"You must have some ideas," said Liam.

"Jake thinks I should do cartwheels or juggle," said Paddy, making a face.

"Well, I know you can't do cartwheels but you can juggle," agreed Liam. "You're a very good juggler."

"But I have to learn something new!" pouted Paddy, going to sit on the other swing.

"Well then, why don't you walk on stilts *and* do your juggling?" replied Liam.

"At the same time?" Paddy asked fearfully.

"Yes, at the same time!" laughed Liam. "You have lots of time to practise. It shouldn't be that hard."

"I don't know how to walk on stilts," said Paddy.

"I'll loan you mine. I'll even help you," his cousin offered.

"Juggling *and* stilt walking … at the same time?" Paddy said slowly. "That sounds very hard."

"It would be a really cool thing to do," agreed Jake.

"You'll see. It's not as hard as you think," said Liam, turning to walk away. "Come on, let's go over to my house. Mom and Dad will be happy to see you, Paddy."

As they walked, they talked about the parade.

"Did you know that my little brother, Shaun, is the band leader this year?" asked Liam.

"No," replied Paddy, not very interested.

"He's very excited about wearing his band uniform with the tall hat!" laughed Liam. "I'll be walking on my really high stilts. The parade is going to be a blast."

"I sure hope so," mumbled Paddy. He was too worried to even think of having fun.

All afternoon Jake and Liam worked on Paddy. Finally, he agreed to try the stilts if Liam would help.

For the next three weeks, Paddy practised every day. Liam helped him, too. At last, Paddy became more

confident. When he wasn't using the stilts, he practis.
with his juggling balls.

But Paddy knew the hard part was still to come. He
would soon have to do them both together.

Chapter 2

Paddy's Friends

School was over at last and all over Fairyland, everyone was getting ready for the parade. It was now less than two weeks away.

Paddy was sitting on his front steps and Jake flew by and saw him. He landed on Paddy's shoulder.

"What's wrong, Paddy?" he asked. "You look so unhappy."

"This is harder than I thought," mumbled Paddy, kicking the stilts.

"Have you been practising?" asked the blue and green parrot.

"Yes! A lot!" declared the leprechaun. "But it's still hard, Jake.

Their friend, Tara, the magic butterfly, came by and landed on a flower.

"Come on, Paddy. You have to stop worrying. You can do it," she said. Tara was able to read thoughts. She knew he was having a hard time.

"Do you really think so, Tara?" asked Paddy.

"I know you can," she replied. "You just have to keep

practising, Paddy. But there is something else you should know."

"Something else?" asked Paddy.

"Yes, you have to believe in yourself," she said.

Paddy frowned.

"What do you mean, believe in myself?"

"Well, if you think you *can't* do it, then you won't!" exclaimed Tara. "You *must* believe you can. Then it will be much easier, you'll see. Remember your math last year, Paddy?"

"Yes … when I practised more, it got easier," Paddy admitted.

"The math wasn't really getting easier," explained Tara. "You practised so much you just learned it. You became more confident, too."

"Tara's right, Paddy!" squawked Jake. "Try it!"

"This is very different than math. I know it won't work for stilts!" groaned Paddy.

"You must stop thinking like that, Paddy," said Tara. "If you don't, it will never happen. I have to go now. You don't have much time to waste. Parade day is only ten days away."

Tara flew into the air. She pretended to fly away, but she stopped at a nearby tree. She wanted to see what Paddy was going to do. *Should I use my magic fairy dust to help him?* she thought. But she knew it would be better for Paddy to do this on his own.

"Come on Paddy, try it ... please!" Jake pleaded, flying around and around above him. "You *can* do it. I know you can."

Paddy buckled on his stilts. Holding onto the railing, he stood up. He carefully got his balance. Then he walked to the end of the sidewalk. He turned around. Taking the balls from his pocket, he tried to smile.

I can do it! I can do it! he repeated to himself.

He threw one ball into the air and caught it. Then he

put a ball in each hand. He threw them into the air and caught them with the other hand. He did it again, and again.

I can do it! I can do it! he said to himself.

Finally, he threw the third ball into the air. He tossed the balls once ... twice ... three ...

"Oh no!" Jake cried as Paddy missed one of the balls.

Paddy tried to catch it but the ball fell onto the grass. Then his stilts began to wobble.

The second ball fell, too. It bounced along the sidewalk. He took another wobbly step, but it was no use. He fell with a thud onto the grass.

"No way! This is too hard!" he cried.

"CAREFUL, PADDY!" said a deep voice by his left hand. "You almost squished me! Are you having trouble?"

Paddy peered into the grass.

"I'm sorry, Mister Grasshopper. You're sure lucky you don't have to use stilts."

"Oh I don't know about that, Paddy," laughed the old grasshopper. "If these stiff old legs worked better, I'd try those stilts. It looks like fun!"

Jake flew down to join them.

"Hello Mister Grasshopper. Come on, Paddy. Let's try it again. You did really well," he encouraged his friend.

"Yes, go on, Paddy. I'll cheer you on, too," said Mister Grasshopper. "Concentrate really hard. You can do it!"

Paddy unbuckled one of the stilts. Jake swooped down toward him. He picked up one of the balls in his beak. Paddy hopped over to the other ball. He put it into the pocket of his vest. Then he hopped over to the steps. He was not very happy.

He was thinking about what Tara and Mister Grasshopper had said. *I wish I could trade places with Mister Grasshopper! Could this really be fun?*

He put his stilt back on and stood up. He balanced himself as Jake flew in closer. Paddy held out his hand

and Jake dropped the ball into it.

"Okay, come on, Paddy. You can do it!" he squawked.

With Tara and Mister Grasshopper watching, Paddy tried again. After many tries and many dropped balls, Paddy did it perfectly! They were all very proud of him.

Paddy is lucky to have such a good friend like Jake, thought Tara. *I think he'll be okay now.* Knowing Paddy was feeling better, she flew away. No one had even noticed her.

"That's enough for today," sighed Paddy, sitting down on the steps. He was suddenly feeling very tired.

"That was really stupendous," squawked Jake.

"Thanks for your help, Jake. Are you thirsty?" asked Paddy. "Let's go see if Mom has made some orange juice."

"Yuck!" replied Jake. "Orange juice is not for this bird. I'll have a drink from the bird bath instead!"

Paddy grinned as he watched Jake fly toward the back yard. He slowly unbuckled his stilts. Actually, he *was* very proud of himself. They were right. He *could* do it. He was almost ready for the parade.

Chapter 3

Band Practice

A few days later, Paddy was at the playground. He was practising on his stilts when Jake flew by.

"The parade is only ten days away, Paddy," the parrot reminded him. "Have you been practicing every day? See I'm practising. I'm in the parade, too!"

As Jake flew away, Paddy saw he was holding some coloured balloons. Jake flew higher then swooped down. He flew in circles above Paddy. He loved to bug his friend by flying too close.

Paddy looked up at Jake, but the bright sunshine blinded him. Paddy blinked. He blinked again. He couldn't even see Jake. Actually, he couldn't see anything. He blinked again. Suddenly, he felt very dizzy. His stilts began to wobble.

"BE CAREFUL, PADDY," squawked Jake. "WATCH WHAT YOU'RE DOING!"

"I'm trying!" cried Paddy. He swayed back and forth. It was no use. He crashed to the ground. One stilt came off banging him on the head.

"OWW! JAKE! That's it!" he cried, sitting on the

ground and rubbing his head. "I've had enough of your tricks! I'm not going to take you on any more moonbeam rides if you can't behave!"

"Gee Paddy! I didn't make you fall. Don't blame me! You have to practise more," cried the parrot. He flapped his wings to control his balloons.

"I'm tired of practicing," Paddy retorted. "I've practised enough!"

"Then don't blame me if you fall again. The bee twins will buzz you with their banner. The band is going to play really loud! I think you should practice some more," warned Jake.

On Monday, Paddy took his stilts and went over to the schoolyard. He knew the leprechaun band was going to practise today. So, he decided to take Jake's advice. He would practise while the band played.

Perfect! he thought, seeing the band members arrive. He buckled on his stilts and began to walk around.

It wasn't long before the band was ready. They lined up in straight rows. Paddy's cousin, Shaun, waved at him. Then Shaun went to stand in front of the band. He blew his whistle and waved his arms about. The drums began to play and the band began to move.

Jake heard the noise and decided to watch from a tree.
This is going to be interesting, he thought.

Billy and Ben, the Bumble Bee twins, had also come to practise. They zoomed overhead. They dipped and dived pulling a long, red banner announcing the fair.

Suddenly, Shaun gave the band the order to play. "BOOM! BOOM! BOOM!" went the big bass drum.

Then all the instruments began to play.

What a noise, thought Jake. He looked over at Paddy but he was already in trouble. The band was so close to him he had missed a step. His stilts were already beginning to wobble. Paddy tried hard to control them.

"OH NO!" Jake squawked, but it was no use. Paddy went crashing to the ground.

Some of the band saw him and stopped playing. Others stopped marching. Soon they were all banging into each other. Shaun blew his whistle. They all stopped, then ran over to see what was wrong.

Jake watched in horror. He flew over Paddy flapping his wings wildly. He was really worried about his friend. He flew down closer to take a look.

Paddy wasn't moving. He just lay there.

Chapter 4

Paddy's Hospital Visit

"Oh, my gosh! Paddy! Are you hurt?" squawked Jake. "Someone call 911. Hurry! Hurry!"

Everyone ran over to see what had happened.

"I WILL," called one of the clarinet players. "I just live over there." He pointed to a house across the street and ran off.

Jake flew down closer to the group.

"GET BACK!" he screeched. "PADDY NEEDS SOME AIR!" He flew back and forth flapping his wings.

Finally, everyone did move back. Paddy was lying very still. His eyes were closed, too.

Shaun went over to see what had happened to his cousin. He knelt down beside him. "Paddy! Wake up Paddy!" he called. "Are you all right?"

Jake flew down and landed on the ground beside his friend. At last, one of Paddy's eyes opened.

"Paddy, are you all right?" asked Jake.

"I … don't … know," Paddy mumbled.

He tried to sit up.

"Oww! My leg hurts!" he moaned.

"Maybe it's broken, Paddy!" said Jake. He really hoped he was wrong.

"He can't have a broken leg," said the trumpet player. "He's the Parade Marshall!"

"Can you move your leg, Paddy?" asked Shaun.

"No, I can't," he groaned. "It really hurts!"

"What's going on here?" asked an adult voice. It was the Band Teacher.

Shaun went over to talk to him.

Just then, they heard a very loud siren. An ambulance roared around the corner. Its red lights were flashing on and off. It pulled up to the curb.

Two Red Cross elves jumped out. One was short and one was tall. The tall one opened the back door and got out a stretcher. He carried it over to Paddy. The elves looked at Paddy's leg and shook their heads sadly.

"We'll have to take you to the hospital," said the short elf, unbuckling Paddy's stilts.

They lifted him onto the stretcher.

"Oww," Paddy groaned again, trying not to cry.

"We'll have you fixed up in no time," said the tall elf. "But you're going to have to be brave."

"I'll try," replied Paddy.

"Good-bye Paddy," called his friends as they carried him away.

"I sure hope it's not broken," mumbled Jake.

The Red Cross elves carried him over to the

ambulance and shut the door. As it roared away, the siren began to scream again.

After dinner, Liam, Shaun and Jake visited Paddy at the Fairyland Hospital. They saw Paddy's parents.

"How is he doing, Aunt Emily?" asked Liam.

"We're glad you've come," said Mr. O'Reilly. "I think Paddy can use some cheering up."

"We'll do our best, Uncle Ryan," grinned Shaun.

When the boys entered the room, they were shocked at what they saw. Paddy was lying in bed with his leg up in the air. There was a big white cast on it. He looked very unhappy despite the balloons and flowers in the room.

"Cheer up, Paddy," said Liam. "They're going to let you be the Parade Marshall next year. You'll have lots of time to practise now."

Paddy rolled his eyes. "I don't want to walk on stilts ever again!" he declared. "My leg hurts!"

They all looked at each other.

"We know, Paddy, and we're really sorry this happened," said Liam. "You were doing so well."

"Gee Paddy. I'll help you next year, too," Jake offered. "You were stupendous!"

"Will you stop with the stupendous!" groaned Paddy.

"I fell and broke my leg. How can that be stupendous?"

"Well, you did look pretty funny," laughed Jake.

Liam gave him a dirty look.

"I'm sorry, Paddy," his friend said quietly. He hid his head under his wing to hide his smile. "You *were* really doing well, honest."

"A fall can happen to anyone," Liam reassured his cousin. "It was an accident and we're really sorry it hurts so much."

"It will get better in a few weeks," said Shaun.

"Everyone is going to think I'm really dumb," mumbled Paddy.

"Come on, cheer up, Paddy. You have to look at the bright side," said Jake.

"And what might that be?" asked Paddy. He couldn't see any bright side to this situation!

"You'll have the coolest looking leg in Fairyland!" squawked Jake.

"That's right," added Shaun. "Everyone will want to sign your cast. Some will even draw pictures on it!"

"That won't make it feel better," grumbled Paddy.

"I think we should let Paddy rest now," said Liam.

He stood up. He and Shaun began to walk to the door.

"Wait a minute!" called Paddy. "Please don't leave yet. I'm more bored than tired. I promise to stop complaining." He sighed a big sigh. "Who is going to be the Parade Marshall now?"

"The Bumble Bee twins are taking your place. They're doing a great job with their banner," said Shaun.

Paddy tried to smile. He realized he *was* feeling a bit sad not to be in the parade.

"I hope I don't miss a Moonrider trip because of my

broken leg," he mumbled.

"The nurse said you'll be out of here tomorrow, Paddy. You're not going to miss anything," Liam assured him. "Now we have to go. We'll see you soon."

"Are you leaving too, Jake?" asked Paddy.

"I'll stay for a few more minutes. All this excitement has made me very tired!" The parrot winked at the boys.

Liam and Shaun laughed as they waved goodbye.

Jake flew over and landed on the end of Paddy's bed. "Well, Paddy, this is sure an interesting way to get out of being Parade Marshall," he said.

"You don't think I did this on purpose, do you?" Paddy exclaimed.

Then he realized his friend was just teasing. He was finally smiling when the nurse came in. She told them that visiting hours were over.

"I'll drop by your house tomorrow, Paddy," called Jake as he flew out the open door.

Chapter 5

Shoe Fairy Family

On a quiet street in Fairyland, the home of the Shoe Fairy family was not being quiet at all. Mr. and Mrs. Shoe Fairy lived in a shoe … yes, they lived in a shoe with their eight children. It was bedtime and eight children can be very noisy. They certainly were tonight.

Eliza, the youngest fairy, was already in bed. She was very unhappy. Hiding under the covers, she began to cry.

"What is the matter, honey?" asked her mother, coming into her room.

"Mommy, I don't have any friends. The other fairies don't like me," Eliza cried.

"That can't be true, dear," said her mother, sitting down on the bed. "Of course they like you."

"No, they don't. They laugh at me."

"Why would they want to laugh at you, dear?"

"They say I'm too small to be of any use."

Then she burst into tears again.

Her mother gave her a hug. "Don't you pay any attention to those silly fairies. They're only jealous that you are so small and pretty."

"Do you think so, Mommy?" asked Eliza.

Her mother gently wiped away her tears. "Yes Eliza, one day you'll find out that being small can be very useful. Now, it's time for you to go to sleep."

Mother tucked Eliza's wings carefully under the blankets and kissed her nose. She turned out the light and quietly left the room. She knew that Eliza would have to grow up some more before she would understand.

You see, Eliza's family had been shoe fairies for a very long time. Their job is to help people who have new shoes. New shoes are often too tight to wear. So a shoe fairy climbs inside the shoe and makes it fit better.

However, in Fairyland, shoes almost never wear out! They magically grow as the feet get bigger. Shoes in Fairyland can last forever!

So, shoe fairies don't have much work to do. Sometimes they visit other places, just like Moonbeam Riders. But Eliza is too young.

The next day, the fairies teased Eliza again. She got so mad she flew away and hid.

"They wouldn't pick on me if I was important," she pouted. "I just have to think of something."

Chapter 6

The Parade

When Paddy awoke on Saturday, the sun was shining. It was a perfect day for a parade.

His leg was feeling much better now but he hated using crutches. When his family finished eating breakfast, they went off to town. Mom carried the picnic basket. Dad carried the folding chairs.

It was a very long walk. Paddy was glad when they found a place to sit down. His arms were so sore. Some of his friends were sitting across the street. They saw him and waved. Paddy waved back. They were all looking down the street. Soon the parade would begin.

Then he saw them! First, the caterpillar clowns came along. Their antics made everyone laugh. Liam went by on his tallest stilts and waved to him. Jake buzzed them with his balloons!

At last, a band could be heard in the distance.

30

The parade was coming! Shaun's band was in the lead. There were many colourful floats. The ant choir was on a large float. One of the ants played the piano. Another played the drums. The whole choir was singing loudly. They were having a blast.

Everyone clapped and cheered as the bands and floats went by. The bee twins dipped and dived as they flew by with their banner. They were doing an excellent job as Parade Marshall.

Paddy really tried to enjoy the parade. Watching everyone else have fun was hard for him at first. But soon he was laughing along with everyone else.

When it was over, his friends came to see him.

"We're sorry you broke your leg, Paddy. Can we sign your cast?" asked Eddie Elf.

Paddy's father handed him a pen. Two of the leprechauns signed their names and Eddie drew a silly picture. They all laughed as they helped Paddy get up.

Jake was right, thought Paddy. I *do have the coolest looking leg in Fairyland! Being Parade Marshall might have been fun, after all!*

"Hey! Are you guys coming?" called Casey Cricket, hopping over to join them. "Are you coming to the fair with us, Paddy? We'll wait for you."

"Yes, I'm coming," he replied happily. He said goodbye to his parents and hobbled after his friends.

Chapter 7

Fairies at Work

When the parade was over, Eliza also said goodbye to her family. Before she could go to the fair, she had something to do. Flying across the street, she went into the Community Centre. Four fairies were waiting for her.

"Come on, let's hurry," said Charlene, the oldest fairy. "I want to go to the fair."

"Me, too," said Eliza.

Charlene took them into one of the meeting rooms. On a long table were rows and rows of backpacks. They belonged to the Moonbeam Riders.

"The Riders will need these today," Charlene explained. "Each backpack must have a new supply of magic fairy dust and fairy buttons."

"It shouldn't take long if we hurry," said Annie, one of the other fairies. "There's a new ride at the fair this year. It looks too cool! I can't wait to try it out."

As they worked, Eliza forgot all about the fair. Her mind was on other things … important things. Eliza had thought up a brilliant idea.

If I climb inside one of these backpacks, I could be a Moonbeam Rider, too! she thought.

She grew very excited and worked even faster. She tried not to think about it. But she couldn't get it off her mind.

An hour later, they were finished. The other fairies left in a big hurry. Eliza flew to the door and looked back.

I'm so small no one will even see me, she thought. *I'll be back before bedtime.*

She flew over to the table and landed on one of the backpacks. Before she could change her mind, she jumped in. She bounced about until she came to rest on something soft. It was the pouch of fairy dust.

"I wonder what they use this for? ACHOO!" she sneezed, as the dust tickled her nose.

It was very dark inside the backpack. Eliza sat down to wait. Before she could stop herself, she had fallen asleep.

Chapter 8

Moonbeam Riders

A bit later, in her castle high among the stars, the Fairy Queen received a special message.

"Where is Janna?" she exclaimed, picking up the fairy phone. "I need to get a message to Mister Cricket right away."

Five minutes later, Janna, the fairy messenger, was flying over the fairground. She was looking for Mister Cricket. At last, she found him at the band concert. She flew down and landed on his shoulder.

"Mister Cricket!" she shouted into his ear in her tiny voice. "The Fairy Queen needs the Moonbeam Riders right away."

When the band finished their song, Mister Cricket went up to the front. Climbing onto a toadstool, he waved to the crowd. Everybody stopped talking. They knew it must be something important.

"The Fairy Queen has sent an urgent message for the Moonbeam Riders," said Mister Cricket. "Many Earth children seem to be having problems today. All the

Moonbeam Riders are needed immediately. You must go to the Community Centre NOW!"

There was great excitement. Crickets, elves, leprechauns and fairies hurried toward the exit. Janna gave each of them a blank sheet of paper.

As they held the paper in their hand, letters magically appeared. It told them which moonbeam to catch and where. It also told them the name and address of the child they were going to visit.

Mister Cricket stopped Paddy at the exit.

"Paddy ... I mean, Mister Moonbeam." (He had almost forgotten the Fairy Queen had given Paddy a new name.) "I'm afraid you're not going to be able to travel on moonbeams with that broken leg," he said.

"Sure I can, Mister Cricket," Paddy replied. "I can tie my crutches on the moonbeam. Jake will help me, too."

"You'll have to be very careful," warned Mister Cricket. "You must hold onto the moonbeam very tightly. Jake, you will take care of him, won't you?"

"Yes, Mister Cricket. We'll be very careful," squawked Jake.

Paddy grinned as Jake landed on his shoulder.

Paddy took the paper from Janna. "We catch *Moonbeam Number 21* today, Jake. We're going to visit

Shayla in Yellowknife, Canada."

"Yellowknife! I thought Shayla lived in Calgary, Alberta?" replied Jake.

"Yes, she did, but she's moved to Yellowknife. That's in the Northwest Territories. It's quite a bit farther north than Calgary. She's almost up at the North Pole!" said Paddy.

"Oh boy! I like going to Shayla's house," Jake exclaimed. "She has a big dog. Will it be all snowy up there, Paddy? Brrr, will we need our warm coats?"

Paddy waggled his finger sternly at his friend.

"First of all, I don't want you to tease Shayla's dog. If he barks, it will wake up the whole family! And no, the snow should be gone by now. It's June remember? Yes, they do get a lot of snow in Yellowknife. I'm very glad she hasn't called us in the winter!"

"You're always spoiling my fun," Jake pouted, not really listening to what Paddy was saying.

"If you're going to be a Moonbeam Rider, Jake, you must act responsibly," Paddy reminded him.

Sulking, the blue and green parrot tucked his head under his wing. Then he flew ahead of Paddy.

"Mister Moonbeam and Jake!" buzzed Mrs. Bumble Bee. She swished her scary-looking stinger back and forth. "You two had better hurry. This is no time for a silly argument."

"We're just getting our backpack, Mrs. Bee," exclaimed Paddy, hobbling after Jake. "We'll hurry."

The other Moonbeam Riders had already picked up their backpacks. There was only one left. Paddy set his crutches down and put it on.

"Off you go now," buzzed Mrs. Bee. "Hurry, hurry! They're calling your number."

"Moonbeam Number 21 ... Number 21," a voice called. "All aboard for Yellowknife, Northwest Territories!"

Chapter 9

A Seagull Named Georgio

Eliza Shoe Fairy suddenly woke up. She was confused. She wondered where she was. It was very dark. She felt a bump and banged into something hard.

"OUCH!" she cried. Then Eliza remembered. She was in one of the Moonbeam Rider backpacks. Someone must have picked it up.

She bumped against something else and rolled over and over. Finally, she found something to hold onto.

She could hear voices talking. She wondered who was wearing her backpack. As they bumped along, Eliza

thought about what she was doing. She had wanted to be a Moonbeam Rider so badly, but now she wasn't so sure.

"What is Mommy going to say?" she said out loud. "She will notice that I'm missing. I know she will. I'm going to be in a lot of trouble when I get home. I don't think this was such a good idea after all."

The bumping stopped. She listened but she couldn't

hear anything. *Do I want to get out?* she thought. *This could be my last chance.*

She could see some light coming from a small hole above her. She flew toward it.

"Help," she called. "Help! Please let me out!"

She pulled on the top of the backpack. Then she heard a voice.

"ALL ABOARD," it called.

She had heard that voice before. It was the moonbeam. They were about to leave. She had to hurry.

"Please let me out!" she called, poking her head outside of the hole.

Suddenly, they began to move. She fell … down … down … down into the backpack.

"Oww!" she sobbed, beginning to cry. "It's no use. They can't hear me. I'm just too small." As they bounced along, she found something soft. "This feels like the bag of fairy dust. Mom and Dad are going to be really mad at me this time."

But there was nothing she could do. She was going to be a Moonbeam Rider … just like she had wanted!

Paddy climbed onto the moonbeam. After putting his crutches away safely, he sat down.

"Hold on tight, Jake," he warned his friend. Jake

grasped his shoulder trying not to claw him.

Then they were on their way. Clouds flashed past the moonbeam as it zoomed toward earth. Suddenly, Jake squawked in alarm. The wind was too strong. It was pulling and pulling at him. His claws were beginning to slip!

Paddy noticed it, too. He held on even tighter to the moonbeam. The wind pulled at his hat. He grabbed it, but he had to let go of the moonbeam.

Another gust of wind pulled at Paddy's coat.

Uh, oh! Paddy and Jake are in trouble! First, his hat flies away. Then, they tumble off the moonbeam.

The Fairy Queen watched the Moonbeam Riders through her magic window. One by one, they safely left Fairyland.

"Oh my!" she cried, as Paddy and Jake tumbled off into space. "Is there no end to the trouble these two can find? I had so hoped Paddy would learn to be more responsible. That's why I gave him the name, Mister Moonbeam."

But the Fairy Queen didn't need to worry. Flying just below them was a bird. But this was no ordinary bird. This was Georgio, the magic seagull.

Georgio saw Paddy's hat as it sailed past him. He swooped down and caught it in his beak. Wondering where it had come from, he looked up. Something green was coming toward him through the clouds. It was coming fast!

It's one of those silly Moonbeam Riders, thought Georgio. *They're always falling off their moonbeams!*

He knew he had to act quickly. If he didn't, there would be a very unhappy child on Earth tonight.

Georgio quickly made himself bigger … MUCH BIGGER! Actually, he grew quite huge! He quickly flew underneath them. Spreading his huge wings, the Moonbeam Riders fell safely onto his back.

It came as quite a shock to Paddy when he landed on something soft. It didn't feel like the moonbeam at all.

Looking down he saw long white feathers.

"We've landed on a big bird, Jake!" he called, looking around. "WHERE ARE YOU, JAKE?"

"He's right behind you," Georgio called. "Hey, I'm no ordinary bird, thank you. I'm Georgio, the seagull. It looks like you have a problem. Is that a broken leg you've got, Moonbeam Rider?"

"Yes, I have. So what!" snapped Paddy. He wasn't surprised at all to see a talking bird. In his world, there were many magical things.

"Now I've seen everything!" laughed Georgio. "A Moonbeam Rider with a broken leg!"

"I've never seen such a large seagull, so we're even!"

Paddy declared. "Georgio, we need …."

Jake's claws dug into his arm.

"Ouch! Jake, are you all right?"

"Yes, I'm okay!" squawked the parrot.

"We need to catch our moonbeam, Mister Seagull," Paddy cried. "Can you help us?"

"Don't worry. I see it! I'll have you there in a jif," called Georgio.

Paddy and Jake held on for dear life. The seagull flapped his huge wings. They soared through the clouds after their moonbeam.

Jake was the first to notice the moving lights in the dark sky. "What are those coloured clouds?"

"They're called Northern Lights. You can only see them in northern countries. Pretty aren't they? Too bad we can't stay up here for awhile. They put on quite a light show. Better get ready to jump!" Georgio called, as the moonbeam got closer.

"We need some help, Mister Bird," called Jake. "Paddy can't jump very well!"

"I've got it covered!" called Georgio. He flew up beside the moonbeam and flicked his tail.

Paddy and Jake found themselves flying through the air. They felt like acrobats. They landed right in the middle of the moonbeam.

"Where have you two been?" asked the moonbeam. "We're almost there!"

"Never mind!" snapped Paddy. "THANKS, GEORGIO. THAT WAS AWESOME!"

"WE MADE IT! THANKS, BIRD!" squawked Jake.

"ANY TIME!" the seagull called back, circling overhead. He quickly made himself smaller, winked at them and flew off.

Paddy and Jake couldn't believe their eyes. Then Paddy remembered they were about to land. He quickly looked down to see where they were. He could see the lights of Yellowknife. They were getting bigger and bigger.

"We're going to land," he called. "Hold on, Jake!"

With a thud, they landed on the window sill.

"This must be Shayla's new home," said Paddy, picking up his crutches. "Let's go!"

They quickly slid into Shayla's dream.

Shayla stirred and turned over.

Jake was so happy to see Shayla and know they were safe.

"Where's the dog?" he squawked.

Shayla smiled in her dream world. She knew her Fairyland friends had arrived.

Chapter 10

Shayla's Problem

Earlier that evening, seven-year-old Shayla and her dog, Rev, were playing in her room. Spring had finally arrived in Yellowknife, but Shayla was still unhappy.

Rev knew she had a problem. He also knew how she could solve it. He wished he could help her, but he couldn't talk.

Suddenly, Shayla jumped up.

"Rev! I know who can help me," she said excitedly, giving the dog a hug. "I had completely forgotten about Mister …."

"Woof! Woof!" barked Rev, warning her to be quiet. She had finally remembered, but it was their secret.

"Do you remember, boy? Mister Moonbeam and Jake can help me!" Shayla whispered. "The leprechaun gave me the Magic Fairy Button? He told me …."

"Woof! Woof!" barked Rev again. He went over to the door and nudged it shut. *It could be very difficult to explain this to her mother,* he thought.

Shayla opened the top drawer of her dresser. Lifting the lid of her jewellry box, she took out the blue button—the one with the cute little fairy on it. Mister Moonbeam had given it to her on his first visit. He had called it a Magic Fairy Button. She had almost forgotten she had it.

"He told me to use it if I had a problem. I have to hold it in my hand when I fall asleep. They will come into my dream and help me again."

"Woof! Woof!" barked Rev, softly. *Now put the button away, Shayla. You don't want to lose it.* He was thinking very hard hoping Shayla would hear him.

Shayla looked at the button and grinned. Then, she put it back into her jewellry box and shut the drawer.

Just then, her mother knocked on the door. She came into the room.

"It's time you two got ready for bed," she announced. "You have school in the morning, Shayla."

"Ok, Mom. I won't be long. I don't think I will read tonight. I'm kind of tired. Come on, Rev. I'll put you outside while I scrub my teeth."

Mother watched them go toward the door. She was puzzled. It wasn't at all like Shayla to go to bed so quickly. She always liked to read a story first.

Shayla put Rev outside and went to scrub her teeth. Then she quickly got into her PJs. She was so excited. She could hardly wait to go to sleep.

"Mister Moonbeam is coming!" she sang quietly.

She heard Rev bark and ran to the front door to let him in.

Rev followed her into the bedroom. She wrapped her arms around his big soft neck and hugged him.

"Good-night, Rev. I'm sorry you can't sleep in my room. I'll tell you all about my dream in the morning."

Rev went out and she shut the door.

She went over to her dresser drawer and got the Magic Fairy Button. She thought about Mister Moonbeam's instructions. She climbed into bed and put the button under her pillow. There was a knock at the door and her mother came in.

"Ready for bed already, honey?" her mother asked. She sat down on the side of Shayla's bed. "You must be tired. I've never seen you so eager to go to sleep."

They hugged each other and her mother pulled the blankets up under Shayla's chin.

"Happy dreams!" she said, as she walked to the door.

Shayla smiled and closed her eyes. The door clicked shut. She reached under her pillow for the button.

Suddenly, she felt very tired.

"Please come and visit me tonight, Mister Moonbeam," she whispered. She held the button tightly in her hand. In no time at all, she was fast asleep.

Chapter 11

Earth Visitors

As Shayla lay asleep that night, she did have a dream. And into her dream came her special visitors.

"Is that you, Mister Moonbeam? Are you really here?" she whispered. "Is Jake with you?"

"Yes, Shayla we're both here," Paddy said softly, rubbing his sore leg. He looked around for a place to sit down.

"Paddy, Paddy!" Jake screamed as he flew around the room. "We had better be quick. The moonbeam is coming back already."

"It's all right, Jake. We just got here! Now, be quiet so I can talk to Shayla."

He unhooked his magic walking stick from his belt. Holding his crutches in the other hand, he sailed across the room. Landing on Shayla's dresser, he put down his crutches. He took off his backpack and sat down.

"Shayla, you can tell me your problem now. You

must be quick," he urged her. "Is it a problem with Rev? Has he been naughty? Are you having trouble at school?"

"No! Nothing like that!" she replied, sitting up. Then she saw Paddy's cast. "What happened to your leg, Mister Moonbeam?"

"I had a little accident that's all, Shayla. Now tell me about your problem," he repeated.

"It's my bike," she replied, still wondering about his leg.

"What's a bike?" squawked Jake. "Where is it? I'll help you find it."

"Be quiet, you silly parrot! She means her bicycle." Mister Moonbeam shook a finger at his friend. "We don't have much time, Jake." He turned back to face Shayla. "What's wrong with your bicycle?"

"It's too hard to ride. It keeps falling over!" she exclaimed.

"Have you been practising, Shayla? Sometimes we just have to learn by doing it over and over again. That's how I broke my leg. I needed more practise walking on my stilts!" He looked over at Jake and winked.

Shayla giggled.

"I have been practising," she replied. "I've tried to

ride my bike so many times. The winter is very long here. I can't ride my bike in the snow. By the time I learn to ride, summer will be over again!"

"Hmm, I see what you mean. Do you have training wheels, Shayla?" asked Mister Moonbeam.

Shayla nodded. "But it still falls over! Please, help me, Mister Moonbeam?"

Paddy looked over at the window. He would have to hurry. Jake was right, the moonbeam *was* coming.

Jake flew back to the window. He hopped up and down on the windowsill flapping his wings. *We're going to miss the moonbeam if Paddy doesn't hurry!*

Mister Moonbeam pointed his walking stick toward the window and landed beside Jake.

"I have the perfect answer, my feathered friend. We'll sprinkle Shayla's bedroom with fairy dust. When she wakes up tomorrow her first wish will be granted."

"That's a stupendous idea!" exclaimed Jake.

Paddy pointed his walking stick again and landed back on the dresser.

"Yes, Shayla, I think we can help you," he said.

But Shayla didn't hear him. She had gone back to sleep and was dreaming about leprechauns and fairies.

Opening his backpack, Paddy searched for the pouch of magic fairy dust. "There has to be some fairy dust in here somewhere."

Eliza was sitting in the bottom of the backpack

shaking with fear. She didn't know what to do. She watched a hand reach into the bag. She barely managed to stay away from it.

Suddenly, two dark eyes peered down at her. *It's Mister Moonbeam and Jake!* she thought. *I'm in Mister Moonbeam's backpack.* She covered her face with her hands and held her breath.

"Wait! I found it, I found it!" he cried, holding up the pouch. "Now hurry, Jake. Fly around the room and sprinkle it over everything."

Jake took the little bag and circled the room, flapping his wings madly. As he flew around, bits of sparkling dust fell out of the bag. As they floated in the air, they twinkled brightly.

Meanwhile, Eliza carefully climbed up to the top of the backpack and looked out. Jake and Paddy were too busy to notice.

She flew out and landed on Shayla's bed. Suddenly, she stopped. There were eyes watching her ... many eyes! *Oh no,* she thought. *I don't like this at all!* She quickly hid. Then very slowly, she peeked around the corner. In the dim light, she could see some shapes behind those eyes.

They're not moving, she thought. Carefully she reached out to touch one of them. *It's very soft—just like my stuffed toys at home—only it's much bigger. That's what they are. They're Shayla's toys! No wonder they're so big.* She sat down on a soft, white teddy bear. It felt just like the one she had at home.

Jake finished sprinkling the fairy dust and landed beside Paddy. Quickly, they repacked the backpack. That is, everything except Eliza ... she was fast asleep on the teddy bear.

Jake flew back to the window.

"Here it comes!" he squawked. "Hurry, Paddy!"

The moonbeam landed on the windowsill lighting up the room. Paddy quickly put on his backpack. He picked up his crutches and took one last look at Shayla.

He waved his magic walking stick in the air. He and Jake slipped out of Shayla's dream and landed on the moonbeam.

The bright light woke Eliza up. She looked around. The backpack had disappeared. Mister Moonbeam and Jake had also disappeared.

She could hear them talking but she couldn't find them. She flew over to the window.

"Sweet dreams, Shayla," she heard them call.

"Wait for me, Mister Moonbeam. Please, wait for me!" Eliza called. "I want to go home, too."

She looked out the window and saw them. She banged her fists on the glass. But she was too late. The moonbeam had already disappeared.

Chapter 12

Eliza

Eliza sat down on the windowsill and began to cry. "What am I going to do now?" she sobbed. A few minutes later, she wiped her tears and looked around.

I guess I will have to be brave, she thought. In the dim light, she looked over at Shayla. She was still sleeping. This was the first Earth person she had ever seen. *She is very big!*

All of a sudden, she heard a strange sound. It was coming from near the door. *It sounds like an elf crying, but that can't be possible!* she thought.

She flew around the room again. It was so dark she couldn't see very well. Suddenly, there was a bump at the door. "Who is it?" she asked, but the noise stopped. She flew over Shayla's bed. She knew she must not wake her, but what was that noise? She landed on a teddy bear sitting on the floor.

Shayla sure likes stuffed animals! she thought. *She*

must be a nice Earth person. I wonder if she will be able to see me?

All of a sudden, she spotted something else.

"Is that a shoe?" she said out loud, forgetting to be quiet. She flew over to Shayla's soft, furry slipper. *It looks sort-of like a shoe. I'd feel much better if I can sleep in a shoe,"* she thought.

She studied it carefully without going too close. Then bravely, she flew inside.

"Ahhh," she yawned, lying down in the soft fur. "It's so cozy and dark in here."

She yawned again. In no time at all, she was fast asleep. This time, she didn't hear Rev crying at the door.

When Paddy and Jake arrived back in Fairyland, they found the fair was over. Elves and gnomes in white overalls were putting everything away.

"I want to see what happens. I want to see Shayla ride her bike," Jake squawked excitedly.

"Yes, I do, too. We'll go get the magic binoculars. But it won't be morning at Shayla's for a few hours."

Chapter 13

The Wish

The sound of Shayla's alarm clock broke the stillness. Sleepily, Shayla reached over and turned it off. In her slipper, the little shoe fairy heard the alarm, too.

"Oh goodness, what is that awful noise?" she exclaimed, forgetting to be quiet. "It's not the same noise I heard last night."

Rev heard the alarm, too. He poked his head through the now open door. He knew he had heard something in this room last night. It had sounded like a voice—a very small voice. He had not heard anything like it before. He looked around but couldn't see anything.

"Hi Rev. Is it morning already?" Shayla asked sleepily, sitting up in bed. She rubbed her eyes.

Forgetting about the strange voice, Rev barked softly. He was always happy when Shayla woke up. He went over and licked her hand.

"Oh Rev, you're such a good dog," she exclaimed.

"Ouch!" screamed Eliza. Rev had stepped on Shayla's slipper.

The dog's ears perked up. He looked down at the

slipper. He put his nose inside and sniffed. He pushed it along the floor. But Eliza had already flown away.

"Are you trying to tell me to put my slippers on, Rev?" asked Shayla, wrapping her arms around his neck. "You are such a smart dog. I sure wish you could talk."

"Whoof!" he barked. "I can talk, Shayla!"

"WHAT!" Shayla screeched, jumping up in surprise. She stared at her big dog. "Am I dreaming, Rev, or did you just talk to me?"

"If you heard me, I guess I'm talking," the dog exclaimed.

"How did that happen?" she asked, sitting down on the floor beside him.

"I don't know, but isn't it great?" Rev said excitedly. "Hurry up and get dressed. Let's go outside and play!"

"Shayla! It's time to get up," called mother. "Don't forget to feed Rev."

"I haven't forgotten, Mom." *Hmm, I always wondered what Rev was thinking when I didn't feed him.* "Are you hungry, Rev?" she asked.

"As a matter of fact, I am," Rev replied. "Dinner was a long time ago!" He moved around the room sniffing as he went. *I know I heard that voice again*, he thought.

"You don't act very hungry, Rev. I'll get dressed and then feed you," she decided.

As she got dressed, Rev sniffed around Shayla's bed. He even moved some of her things about with his nose.

"Hey, quit that will you!" said the little voice.

There it is again! thought Rev, forgetting he could talk. He moved to the end of the bed.

"Keep that nose to yourself! You're getting my dress all wet!" scolded the voice.

Rev sat down and looked all around. This was a mystery. He knew there was something else in the room, but what? Suddenly, he saw something move in the doll house. He got closer and looked through the small window.

"Sniff, sniff."

Yes, he could smell something all right. He hadn't smelled a smell like this before. He put his nose through the window and sniffed really hard.

"S-NIIII-FFFF!"

"Hey! Stop that you … you thing!" cried the voice.

It called me a thing! thought Rev. But before he could tell Shayla, something tickled his nose.

"AA-CHOO!!"

"Rev, what are you doing?" called Shayla, as she pulled on her socks.

"Something was in your slipper," said Rev. "Then it was in the doll house. It seems to be a little person!"

"A little person? In the doll house?" she asked. "Are you sure it wasn't one of my dolls?"

"Woof!" barked Rev. "No! This one talks! It called me a thing!"

"My goodness, everything in my room seems to be able to talk this morning," said Shayla. "I wonder what is going on here?"

Up in Fairyland, Paddy was watching with the magic binoculars. He was puzzled, too. This was not going according to their plan at all. Rev was not supposed to be talking.

"What are they doing?" asked Jake.

"I don't know, but it's not going right. Darn it anyway!" exclaimed Paddy. "Everything is going wrong. Shayla has used up her wish and now she has a talking dog!"

Jake began to laugh. "A talking dog!" He laughed so hard he had to sit down. He laughed until his tears made his feathers wet.

"It's all right, Paddy. Don't you see what has happened?" said the parrot. "Rev will be able to help Shayla now. I bet it will all work out. You wait and see."

"You're probably right, Jake. But there's something else going on down there. Let's be quiet. Perhaps I can figure it out."

Chapter 14

Shayla meets Eliza

"Rev, if there is someone in here, where are they? Maybe I should tell Mom," said Shayla.

Rev went over to the door and nudged it shut.

"No, I don't think that would be a good idea. Let's see if we can figure it out ourselves."

"But you're frightening me. Is there someone in my room?" she asked.

"I really don't think you need to be frightened. It was a very little person with a very little voice," replied Rev.

"What did it say?"

"I don't know. It was too quiet. Just a minute," he said. "I think I can find it."

Shayla watched as Rev lay down on the floor. He put his head under the bed and sniffed really hard.

"S-NIIII-FFFF!"

"Why are you sniffing, Rev?" she asked.

Rev did not answer. He moved to the end of the bed and sniffed again.

"S-NIIII-FFFF!"

Suddenly, something very small and colourful flew

into the air and landed on his nose.

"Rev, what is that on your nose?"

Rev tried to look, but he went cross-eyed.

Shayla giggled.

He shook his head—hard.

"Ahhhhh!" Eliza screamed in surprise, flying into the air.

"Oh look, Rev! It's a little fairy!" Shayla exclaimed.

"Shhh," Rev reminded her.

"Where did she come from?" Shayla whispered.

"Why don't you ask her?" Rev whispered back.

The little fairy flew up to the ceiling. She looked down at them and flapped her wings.

"Are you going to hurt me?" she asked.

Shayla stood up very slowly. She didn't want to frighten the first fairy she had ever seen in her life.

"Oh Rev, isn't she too cute!" she whispered. "Come on, pretty fairy. We promise we won't hurt you." She held out her hand. "Please talk to me. Where did you come from? How did you get here?"

"Whoof," Rev barked softly.

The fairy flew away and landed on a shelf.

"Rev, be quiet. You frightened her," begged Shayla.

"I'm sorry. I just got a bit excited. After all, I am a dog you know!" Rev replied.

Shayla sighed and shook her head.

"Are you two ready for breakfast?" asked her mother as she hurried by the door. "We have to leave soon, Shayla."

"Oh gosh … school! I almost forgot," Shayla replied, looking at Rev. "I'll just be a minute, Mom."

All right. I'll put your breakfast on the table," her mother called on her way to the kitchen. "You haven't fed Rev yet either. That poor dog will be starving."

Shayla went over to the door and closed it quietly.

"No, I don't think this poor dog will starve!" she giggled, patting his back. "We'll have to hurry. Where are you, little fairy?"

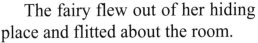

The fairy flew out of her hiding place and flitted about the room.

"Where did you come from?" Shayla whispered.

"I came from Fairyland with Mister Moonbeam," said Eliza in her tiny voice. "He didn't know I was in his backpack. I got out when they weren't looking. They left without me," she said sadly. She flew around the room again. "Now I don't know what to do."

Shayla held out her hand again. This time, the fairy

flew over and landed. Shayla stared at the little creature. She was very pretty but stood only a few inches high.

She had long blonde hair with pink-flower barrettes. Her dress glittered in the light. But it was her wings that really interested Shayla. Their colours were like a rainbow. They were so beautiful.

The little fairy sat down on her hand and began to cry.

"Please don't cry," Shayla begged. "We'll help you get home to Fairyland. Don't worry. All I have to do is call Mister Moonbeam. He'll come back. Of course, I would have liked you to stay for awhile."

The fairy looked up at Shayla and wiped her eyes. Is it really that easy?" she asked. "I would like to stay but my mommy will be very worried."

"That's okay. I understand. I don't like being away from my mom either. It's easy to call Mister Moonbeam. You'll see," said Shayla. "What's your name?"

"My name is Eliza … Eliza Shoe Fairy."

"Shoe Fairy?" repeated Shayla. "That's a different name."

"Is that why you were in Shayla's slipper?" asked Rev. "Do you live in a shoe?"

"Yes, actually I do," said Eliza. "The slipper was very warm and cozy. I must have fallen asleep!"

"Ok, we'll call Mister Moonbeam tonight," said Shayla. "I have to get ready for school now. Can you and

Shayla. "I have to get ready for school now. Can you and Rev get along by yourselves today?" She looked at him sternly.

"I'll be nice to her if she doesn't tickle my nose," he replied. "I'll even give her a ride on my back if she wants. But I don't like being called a thing!"

"I'm sorry, Rev. I didn't know you were a dog then. You are so big—much bigger than Fairyland dogs. I'd like to have a ride on your back," she said, flying around in front of Rev.

"Come on Rev, I'll put some food out for you," Shayla called, going toward the kitchen.

Back in Fairyland, the Shoe Fairy family were looking everywhere for Eliza. But no one knew where she was. Poor Mrs. Shoe Fairy was frantic.

"She can't be very far, mother," said Mister Shoe Fairy. "Perhaps she's got herself locked in somewhere. Someone will find her soon."

"Tell me what's happening at Shayla's house,

Paddy?" asked Jake.

"Everything has gone fuzzy. There must be a storm out there," Paddy replied. "I think I heard Shayla say she was going to call us again tonight. Something strange is going on down there. We might as well go home. If Shayla needs us, the Fairy Queen will let us know."

Paddy put his crutches under his arms and set off. He even forgot to say goodbye to Jake.

Chapter 15

Hide and Seek

Shayla was worried about leaving Rev and Eliza alone. However, she soon got busy and forgot about them.

At home, Rev was asleep on his favourite mat in Shayla's room. On his back, Eliza was sound asleep behind his ear. Suddenly, Rev twitched in his sleep.

Eliza rolled off onto the floor. She landed on the mat beside Rev. Sitting up, she rubbed her head then flew into the air to see what was happening. Rev snored.

"For goodness sake!" she declared. "Rev sounds just like our neighbour, Mister Elf! He snores so loudly I can hear him from across the street! Wake up, dog!" she called into his ear.

But Rev didn't hear her. So, she tried again.

"WAKE UP, REV!" she screamed.

Rev snored even louder.

She flew into Rev's ear and tickled him.

He shook his head and Eliza went flying through the air.

"Rev, you're no fun at all!" she cried. "I want someone to play with me."

Rev opened one of his big eyes and looked at her.

"What is your problem?" he asked.

"You said you would play with me," said Eliza.

"Did I say that? Well, what do you want to play?" the dog asked.

"You could give me a ride on your back," she suggested.

"Would you be happy then? Could I go back to sleep after I take you for a ride?" he asked.

"Is that all you do—sleep?" she asked.

"What else is there to do?" he replied.

"We could play hide and seek," said Eliza.

"Don't you think you have a bit of an advantage over me?" he asked. "It's easy for you to hide!"

"Well, yes, but I could pretend that you're small, too!" said Eliza. She flapped her wings happily.

"All right, we'll try it," Rev agreed. "I'll go hide first and you have to find me."

So, for the next two hours Eliza and Rev played hide-and-seek. Then Rev went back into Shayla's room and lay down on the mat.

"You've worn me out, Eliza. I'm going to have a nap now. Everyone will be home for dinner soon. You can find something else to do."

He put his head down and instantly began to snore.

Eliza giggled. "Playing hide-and-seek was fun. Rev sure had a hard time finding me!"

She flew out of the room and into the kitchen. She landed on the window sill.

Everything is so big here, she thought. *It would really be nice to go home where things are the right size. I miss Mommy and Daddy. I even miss my brothers and sisters! Poor Mommy, she must be worried by now.*

Eliza felt so sorry for herself, she wanted to cry. Then she remembered what Shayla had said. *Shayla said it would be easy to get Mister Moonbeam to come back. I sure hope he can come tonight."*

She flew over to Shayla's room. Rev was snoring even louder. She flew into Shayla's slipper.

"It's a lot quieter in here," she said out loud. So, she crawled right down into the toe. She liked the soft fur. It was not long before she was fast asleep, too.

A little while later, Eliza woke up with a start. She was moving. She rolled over and banged against the side of the slipper.

"Help! Help!" she called.

Rev barked. "Woof! Stop Shayla!" he cried.

Eliza looked up at the light and saw two green eyes.

"Is that you, Eliza?" Shayla asked. "I'm sorry! I'm not used to having a shoe fairy for a friend. Are you okay?"

"Oh yes," said Eliza. "Shoe fairies often get squished I'm told. It's part of our job you know. It hasn't happened to me yet because I'm too young to go to work. I'm glad you've come home, Shayla."

"Your job? Oh right, you're a shoe fairy! I'm glad Rev warned me. I don't want to squish you!" Shayla exclaimed. "Was Rev nice to you today?"

"Yes, we played hide and seek for awhile," said Eliza. "But he sleeps an awful lot!"

Shayla giggled. "Hide and seek with Rev?" she laughed. "I wish I could have seen that!"

"Don't laugh," growled Rev. "She had me running all over the house. I could never find her!"

"Eliza," said Shayla, "I get the feeling you're ready to go home."

"If I could please. It's been a very nice visit but …."

"I'll get Mister Moonbeam to come back for you tonight. Don't worry, your mother will understand. You're going to have quite a story to tell when you get home."

Chapter 16

The Bike Ride

The door to Shayla's room opened and her mother poked her head in.

"Shayla, why don't you take Rev outside for some exercise. Dinner won't be ready for awhile."

"Okay, Mom," she replied, and her mother went away. "Want to go for a run, Rev?"

"Woof! That's a good idea," replied Rev, happily wagging his big tail. It banged against the door. "You should try riding your bike."

"That's right. We have to find out if my wish comes true. Let's go check it out," said Shayla.

"Get on my back, Eliza," said Rev, "and hold on!"

Eliza did as she was told. Shayla ran ahead to get her bike out of the garage. They met in the front yard. She put on her helmet and stood looking at her bike.

"Well here goes," she said. "I sure hope Mister Moonbeam's magic works."

She put one foot on the pedal and pushed off. She felt a bit unsteady at first. Then she realized how great it felt

as she sailed down the sidewalk. This time the training wheels did help. She didn't tip over at all.

"LOOK REV, I'M RIDING!" she called.

"Woof, woof," said Rev, racing along beside her. "Woof, woof, woof!"

Eliza couldn't hold on and flew into the air to watch.

At the end of the block, Shayla used her brakes and the bike stopped.

"Whoa, that was awesome!" she exclaimed. "My dream did come true, didn't it Rev?"

"Woof, woof!" barked Rev as he happily ran around the bike wagging his tail.

"Talk to me, Rev. What's the matter, boy?" asked Shayla. She got off her bike and went over to him. She looked in his eyes.

Eliza flew down and landed on Rev's ear.

"Can't you talk anymore, fella?" asked Shayla. "What's wrong, Eliza? Why isn't Rev talking to me?"

"When did Rev start talking, Shayla? Do you think it was Mister Moonbeam who made him talk?" asked the fairy.

"Actually, he did start talking the day after they were here. It was very strange. I only asked Mister Moonbeam to help me ride my bike," she explained. She was trying very hard not to cry. "Then Rev started talking."

"But your wish has been granted," Eliza reminded her. "Maybe Rev was supposed to help you ride your bike.

That could be why he was able to talk."

"You mean, if I couldn't ride my bike, he would still be talking?" cried Shayla. "Oh Rev, I'm so sorry!"

"But riding your bike was very important to you, wasn't it, Shayla?" asked Eliza. "Rev wanted you to ride your bike, too."

"Y-yes," Shayla sniffled. "But it was so nice having Rev talk to me."

"It was fun wasn't it? It might have caused you some trouble though," said Eliza. "I think you should look on the bright side. Dogs aren't supposed to talk. You had the only talking dog on Earth!"

Shayla smiled.

"I suppose you're right," she said, wiping her tears. "Thanks Eliza. I wish you could stay and be my friend."

Just then Shayla heard her name called.

"Come on, Rev, I hear Mom calling. Sit on my handlebars, Eliza. I'll take you for a ride this time," said Shayla, climbing back onto her bike. "We have lots to do before you go home tonight."

As Shayla rode up the street, she thought about Eliza's words and giggled. *The only talking dog on Earth!* She zoomed up to her house and jumped off the bike. *I can't wait to tell Mom that I can ride my bike now. Maybe we can take the training wheels off now!*

As she put her bike away, she thought about what had happened. It was too bad Rev couldn't talk anymore. But now they would be able to ride to the lake and have a lot more fun. She knew Rev would really like that.

Chapter 17

Eliza Goes Home

The next morning when Shayla woke up, she felt something hard in the bed. It was the Magic Fairy Button. She picked it up and giggled.

Last night in her dream, she said goodbye to Eliza.

Mister Moonbeam was really surprised to find the fairy waiting for him. Shayla remembered hearing her little voice calling goodbye as she went back to sleep.

There was a scratching sound at her door. She jumped out of bed and opened it. Rev's big tail wagged so hard it almost knocked her over.

"Well Rev, I guess it's just you and me again, fella!" she said, snuggling against him.

"Woof, woof!" replied Rev, licking her face.

Back in Fairyland, Paddy, Jake and Eliza arrived home to a big surprise. Eliza's whole family was waiting for her at the park.

"How did you know where I was?" Eliza asked as they all rushed over to see her.

"Janna came over to our house," said her oldest sister.

"The Queen saw you with Mister Moonbeam. She sent Janna to tell us," Mother explained. "We were all very worried, Eliza."

"I'm very sorry I worried you, Mommy and Daddy, but I met the nicest Earth girl and her dog. Her name is Shayla. Everything is so BIG on Earth! You should have seen all her stuffed animals!" Eliza talked so fast, the words tumbled out on top of one another.

"We did wonder where you could have gone," said her father. "I'm glad it turned into a nice adventure. You'll have to tell us all about it. HOWEVER," he said sternly, "we do not want you to ever go away like that again!"

"I know, I'm sorry," said Eliza, looking at the ground. "I-I tried to change my mind, b-but it was too late."

"I had a feeling you were up to something," sighed her mother. "I remembered our talk the other night."

"I—I only thought if I became a Moonbeam Rider ...," Eliza began. "It was only for a little while, but they left me behind. I-I just wanted to be important."

"You're always important to us, dear," said her father.

"I know Daddy, but my friends don't think so."

"It's what *you* think that matters, Eliza, not your friends," said her mother, "but look!" Her mother pointed down the street. "It looks like you have some friends after all. I think they want to hear about your adventure!"

Flying toward them was a group of fairies. They were waving and calling her name.

Eliza began to move toward them. Her mother stopped her.

"Eliza, we want you to make us a promise."

"A promise?" she asked.

"Yes, you must promise never to go anywhere without telling us, ever again," said her mother.

"Yes, I promise, Mommy. Now may I go, please?" she asked.

Her parents looked at each other and nodded.

Eliza grinned, then flew off to meet her friends.

The End

We hope you've had fun reading *3 On A Moonbeam*. Did you know that there is another book in this series entitled, *Leprechaun Magic*? It was the first book in the *Moonbeam Series*. It tells how Paddy and Jake become Moonbeam Riders.

Book 1

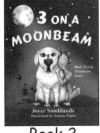
Book 2

Hi Kids,

Remember to tell your teacher and your friends about these books. We love to receive mail from our readers, too. You could visit our website and send us an email.

www.whitlands.com

Whitlands Publishing is proud to publish books for Joyce Sandilands and her bestselling author/husband, J. Robert Whittle.

Turn the page for details on Mr. Whittle's books.

Lizzie Series by J. Robert Whittle (above)
Victoria Chronicles by J. Robert Whittle (below)

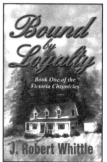

Whitlands Publishing Ltd.
4444 Tremblay Drive
Victoria, BC Canada V8N 4W5 Tel: 250-477-0192
Email: admin@whitlands.com

www.whitlands.com